Christopher Sat Straight Up in Bed

Written by
Kathy Long

Illustrated by
Patricia Cantor

Eerdmans Books for Young Readers
Grand Rapids, Michigan • Cambridge, U.K.

To Keith, Dad,
and Grandpa England with love.
— *K. L.*

To my favorite brave boys: Aaron, Josh, Joe, and Sam.
— *P. C.*

Text © 2013 Kathy Long
Illustrations © 2013 Patricia Cantor

Published in 2013 by Eerdmans Books for Young Readers,
an imprint of Wm. B. Eerdmans Publishing Co.
2140 Oak Industrial Dr. NE
Grand Rapids, Michigan 49505
P.O. Box 163, Cambridge CB3 9PU U.K.

www.eerdmans.com/youngreaders

Manufactured at Tien Wah Press
in Malaysia in August 2012, first printing

13 14 15 16 17 18   9 8 7 6 5 4 3 2 1

Library of Congress Cataloging-in-Publication Data

Long, Kathy.
Christopher sat straight up in bed / by Kathy Long ; illustrated by Patricia Cantor.
p. cm.
Summary: While sleeping over at his grandparents' house,
Christopher hears a very loud, horrible sound during the night
and gets up to investigate whether it is an elephant, a monster, or perhaps a dinosaur.
ISBN 978-0-8028-5359-2 (alk. paper)
[1. Sound — Fiction. 2. Sleepovers — Fiction. 3. Grandparents — Fiction.
4. Snoring — Fiction. 5. Humorous stories.]
I. Cantor, Patricia, 1950–2012 ill. II. Title.
PZ7.L854Chr 2012
[E] — dc23
2011035829

The illustrations were rendered in pastel on sanded paper.
The display type was hand-lettered by Patricia Cantor.
The text type was set in ITC Korinna BT.

FSC
www.fsc.org
MIX
Paper from
responsible sources
FSC® C012700

"What's that?"

Christopher sat straight up in bed.

He watched and waited.

He didn't hear anything else, so he lay back down.

"It must have been a dream," he said.

He closed his eyes.

Then he heard it again.

Honk-Shoo

"What's that?"

Christopher sat straight up in bed again. "It sounds like an elephant trumpeting."

He tiptoed to the window and looked out, but he only saw the moon playing hide-and-seek with the clouds.

Christopher waited and listened. He didn't hear anything else except the squeak of his grandparents' bed. He crawled back into bed and closed his eyes.

Then he heard it again.

Honk-shoo

"What's that?"

Christopher sat straight up in bed again. "Maybe there's a monster under my bed."

He looked under the bed, but he only saw his grandpa's slippers and a bunch of little dust bunnies.

He waited and listened.

The house was quiet, so he crawled back into bed.

Honk-shoo!

"What's that?"

Christopher sat straight up in bed again. "There might be a bear in my closet."

He crept over and opened the closet door. *Squeak!* He only saw his grandpa's shirts hanging in a row and a cowboy hat sitting on the shelf.

He waited, but he didn't hear anything else. So he crawled back into bed.

He wrapped up in the covers.

HoNK-
SHOO!

"What's that?"

Christopher sat straight up in bed again. "It sounds like a dinosaur stomping down the street."

He looked out the window, but he only saw the neighbor's house silent in the moonlight.

"I have to find out what's making that sound!"

So Christopher crawled out
of bed and crept to the door.

He listened.

    No sound.

He waited.

    Still no sound.

He waited a bit more.

Then he heard it again.

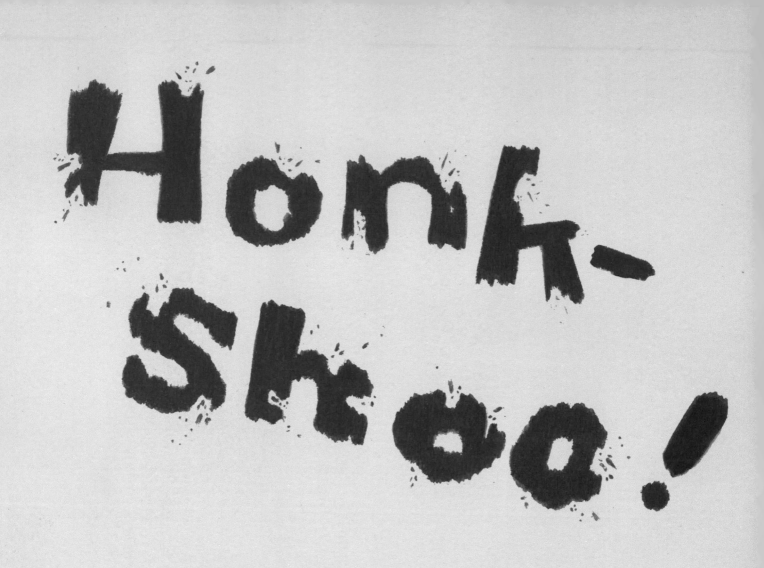

"It's coming from down the hall!"

His heart beat faster.

The shadow of a mountain lion danced on the wall.

He froze.

The shadow moved closer. Christopher's legs wouldn't move.

The shadow looked as if it was going to pounce . . .

Suddenly his grandma's cat jumped out. Christopher jumped back and muffled a scream.

"Oh, Whiskers, it's just you," he laughed.

Then he heard the sound again. It was louder than ever, and the windows shook.

"It's coming from my grandparents' room!"

He continued down the hall and crept through their bedroom door.

"It's coming from my grandparents' bed!"

He tiptoed closer.

SHoo!

"It's coming from my grandpa!"

Grandma poked Grandpa with her elbow. "You're snoring. Roll over," she said.

Grandpa rolled over, mumbling. The bed squeaked.

Christopher laughed. "Grandpa snores — loud!"

"What's that?" Grandma said, and sat straight up in bed.

"What's that?" Grandpa said, and *he* sat straight up in bed.

"It's just me," Christopher said. "I heard something."

"Come on in," Grandma said. "You can sleep with us, but I have to warn you — your grandfather snores."

"So I've heard," Christopher said.

"If he does, poke him and tell him to roll over," Grandma said. "Good night!"

"Good night!" said Christopher.

"Good night!" Grandpa replied.

The house was quiet . . . for a while.

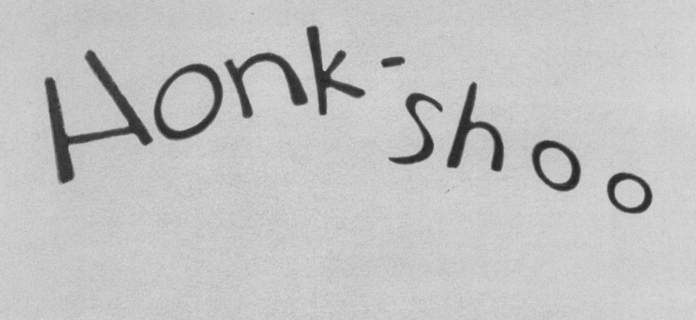

Christopher sat straight up in bed.